WELCOME TO
PASSPORT TO READING
A beginning reader's ticket to a brand-new world!

Every book in this program is designed to build read-along and read-alone skills, level by level, through engaging and enriching stories. As the reader turns each page, he or she will become more confident with new vocabulary, sight words, and comprehension.

These PASSPORT TO READING levels will help you choose the perfect book for every reader.

READING TOGETHER
Read short words in simple sentence structures together to begin a reader's journey.

READING OUT LOUD
Encourage developing readers to sound out words in more complex stories with simple vocabulary.

READING INDEPENDENTLY
Newly independent readers gain confidence reading more complex sentences with higher word counts.

READY TO READ MORE
Readers prepare for chapter books with fewer illustrations and longer paragraphs.

This book features sight words from the educator-supported Dolch Sight Words List. This encourages the reader to recognize commonly used vocabulary words, increasing reading speed and fluency.

For more information, please visit passporttoreadingbooks.com.

Enjoy the journey!

Little, Brown and Company
Hachette Book Group
1290 Avenue of the Americas, New York, NY 10104
Visit us at lb-kids.com
Visit monsterhigh.com

First Edition: February 2017

Little, Brown and Company is a division of Hachette Book Group, Inc. The Little, Brown name and logo are trademarks of Hachette Book Group, Inc.

The publisher is not responsible for websites (or their content) that are not owned by the publisher.

Library of Congress Control Number 2016957649

ISBNs: 978-0-316-54838-0 (pbk.), 978-0-316-54837-3 (ebook)

Printed in the United States of America

CW

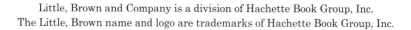

10   9   8   7   6   5   4   3   2   1

The illustrations for this book were created digitally. This book was edited by Kara Sargent and designed by Nic Davies. The production was supervised by Rebecca Westall, and the production editor was Jon Reitzel. The text was set in Century Schoolbook, and the display type is House of Terror.

Passport to Reading titles are leveled by independent reviewers applying the standards developed by Irene Fountas and Gay Su Pinnell in *Matching Books to Readers: Using Leveled Books in Guided Reading*, Heinemann, 1999.

Fierce
Friends

Adapted by
Gina Gold and Margaret Green

Based on the screenplay by
Keith Wagner

Illustrated by
Jessi Sheron

LITTLE, BROWN AND COMPANY
New York   Boston

Frankie Stein could not wait to show her new science project to her ghoulfriends. "It is a super battery!" she said.

Frankie thought it could help
the Normies.

"Why would you want to help the
Normies?" asked Moanica.
"They never help us!"

Clawdeen wanted to help the Normies too.
She wanted to open a salon for monsters and humans!

Frankie liked that idea!
She suggested they turn the
power station into a salon.
The ghouls did not notice that
someone was spying on them...

Moanica was using the power station
for an evil plan.

The Zomboyz told her the ghouls
were coming.

"We have to go underground," she said.

Twyla told Frankie that the Zomboyz
were up to something.
Twyla said she would keep
watching them.

Just then, lightning struck!
Frankie threw herself over
Twyla to protect her.

"Are you okay?" asked Twyla.

"I am fine," said Frankie.

But her bolts were

sparking with electricity.

The next day, Frankie was full of energy from the lightning strike.

"Who broke Frankie?" Clawdeen asked.

Frankie touched the dresses
Clawdeen had made for the salon.
They started to glow.
They looked creeperific!

Frankie shook her hand to get out
the extra electricity.
A ball of energy appeared!
The ghouls called him Znap.

Meanwhile, Twyla followed
the Zomboyz to a cave.
She found out that Moanica
had stolen Frankie's battery!

Moanica said she was going to use
the battery to steal electricity.
She wanted to scare the Normies!
The salon opening would be ruined!

Moanica turned on Frankie's battery.
But it could not hold that much electricity.
It exploded!

Moanica saw that Frankie was
filled with electricity.
She had a new plan.
"Release Twyla!" she told the Zomboyz.

Twyla found Frankie before
the salon opening.
She told Frankie about Moanica's plan.

Frankie had to make sure the salon opening was not ruined. The Normies loved the salon!

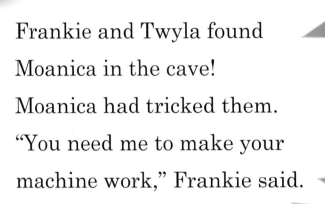

Frankie and Twyla found
Moanica in the cave!
Moanica had tricked them.
"You need me to make your
machine work," Frankie said.

The Zomboyz attached her
to the machine.
Soon, Frankie was filled
with electricity!

All the lights turned off
in Normie Town.
The power station went dark!
Electricity shot through the floor!

Moanica rose up into the salon.

"Are you scared?" she asked the Normies.

"You should be!"

The ghouls found Frankie.

"We have to get all that electricity

out of her," said Draculaura.

"Znap, can you wake her?"

Znap helped Frankie turn all her energy into lots of new znaps. Now they could stop Moanica!

The znaps zoomed into the power lines.
"They are lighting everything back up!"
said Draculaura.

"Thanks, Znap!" said Frankie.

The next day, Clawdeen was sad.
"Nobody is going to come back
to the salon," she said.
"Ghouls, look outside!" said Twyla.

The Normies thought the scare was all
part of the opening.
Frankie was so happy that Clawdeen's
dream was saved!